MW01506407

Grades K–6

A collection of Listening Lessons

MUSiC and magical movement

oh my!

Katie Grace Miller

Editor: Kris Kropff
Book Design: Ashley Donahue

ISBN: 978-0-7877-5854-7

HERITAGE
MUSIC PRESS
A Lorenz Company • www.lorenz.com

Dear Colleague,

I'm so excited to share these ideas of movement with you! I'm confident that your students will enjoy and learn from them because they've been successful in my classroom.

I know that MOVEMENT is in big, bold letters on the cover of this book. And your kiddos will get a *ton* of movement out of these lessons: They will explore their imaginations and stretch the limits of what they can do when it comes to movement. These lessons, however, are as much about listening as they are about movement. The movement is just a vehicle to get students to *actively* listen to these wonderful pieces of music.

Every movement is carefully thought out to complement and showcase the piece that is being listened to. I want students to come away from these activities with not just fun and excitement but also with the ability to describe the music and sounds using music vocabulary and the ability to speak intelligently about what they heard.

At the end of year, I let students pick their favorite lessons to repeat. These activities always make the cut. I hope that they bring your classroom joy year after year as they have mine.

Musically,
Katie Grace Miller

Accessing Digital Files

The form maps and other supporting visuals and resources are available online for download. You can identify them quickly by this icon:

When you see it in the materials list for a lesson, please visit **www.lorenz.com/resources/magical** to find your digital resources.

1. Go to **www.lorenz.com/resources/magical**
2. Type the password provided on page 48.
3. Find the title of the lesson you want, and you will see links to download each file.
4. Or, if you want to download all the files, scroll to the bottom of the page for a link to do so.

contents

Making Magic in Your Classroom

Successful magicians make their shows look effortless and leave everyone wondering "what's the secret?" behind the tricks. Good teachers know that success is never effortless and we work hard to discover and develop secrets along the way. Here are some of my secrets for everything from classroom management to assessments. You'll also find activity-specific tips—Mrs. Miller's Magic Tricks—in each lesson.

The Sound of Silence

Since listening is the primary objective of these lessons, it is imperative that students don't talk during the activity. Before you start let students know that if they are commenting too much during the lesson, you will take away their manipulative. Then, they'll have to earn it back by continuing to participate, silently. No talking is a high standard, but students will rise to it if you set *and* hold students to this expectation from the very beginning. I promise it will be worth it when the behavior follows them from year to year. (And wait until they start correcting each other.)

Magic Words

Each lesson includes a few magic words. Along with giving you a good at-a-glance look at the lesson foci, I encourage you to use these vocabulary words frequently during the lesson. In a few instances I've offered alternatives for younger, or older, students. For a quick in-lesson assessment, you can ask students to "Say the Magic Word." Another assessment idea, "What's the Magic Word?," is offered later in this section.

Visuals

Form maps are provided for each song. These one-page visuals are ideal for projecting but use them in whatever way works best for you—enlarge and print as a poster; use the copy to create your own visual on posterboard; print a copy for each student. Additional supporting visuals are also provided, as indicated within specific lessons. All of these files are available for download at www.lorenz.com/resources/magical and access information is provided on page 2.

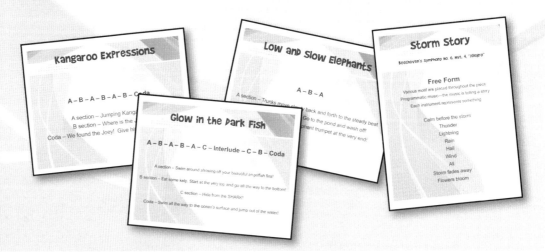

Movement Props

Students love using movement props. Managing how they're used in your classroom will help you love them too.

Parachute

- Don't use the handles. This helps prevent tearing and helps keep everyone at the same level.
- Make sure knuckles are showing, and not thumbs. This will help everyone protect their wrists.
- "Be gentle, it is made out of plastic." Some kiddos get a little out of hand with the shake moves. Remind them about being safe with the parachute.

Ribbon Streamers

- Medium-length streamer are best when it comes to movement. The long ones are usually too long unless you have a huge room and the short ones don't give enough flair to the moves. For me, the 3-foot ribbon streamer sticks are the most successful.

- Instruct students that ribbon streamers should be just that—not swords or light sabers or anything but a ribbon streamer. "And no touching anyone else with your ribbon streamer."
- Proper storage is key to keeping streamers ready to go whenever you're ready to use them. A child-size wooden clothes hanger (with its thicker crossbar) is my go-to storage system. (Thank you Ms. Owen for the giraffe hanger that matches my school's mascot!) Asking students to make sure their streamer is untangled and to hand it to me (so I can quickly drape it over the bottom part of the hanger) also saves time.

Scarves

- "We *do not* put them on our head!" This is a firm rule; you never know who may have lice.

- Anytime I use scarves with my younger kiddos, I try to save a few minutes so we can fold them after the movement activity. It's great motor-control practice (and helps keep the scarves in good condition). We sing the second verse of Lynn Kleiner's "The Colors are Gliding," modifying the lyrics slightly to "folding like this" and "folding like that."

Recordings

Again, these lessons are as much about listening as they are about movement. While much of what students are actively listening for will be audible in any recording, everything they hear will leave an impression. Seek out good recordings of great performers.

Where I have a strong recording preference, I've listed it. At the time of this writing, many of the recommended recordings were available on Spotify. Amazon Prime Music's "basic" level was another good source. And check your public library; many have extensive music collections.

Note that the lessons with very specific timings are based on my preferred recording of the piece. You'll need to be especially careful in prepping these lessons if you use a different version.

Composer Corner

For years I had every intention of doing a composer corner bulletin board. I would make it about three weeks before I'd get overwhelmed by the year. I'd either stop doing it or I'd put "something" on the board but forget to reference it with my students. I finally had a heart to heart with myself: "Katie Grace, you need to get your head in the game, stop brushing aside these important people, and teach these kiddos who's behind all this great music!" I came away a few key realizations.

Rotate every *other* week

Posting a new bulletin board every week is a lot of work, and a lot of pressure. Changing my board every two weeks alleviated some of that pressure. More importantly, it allowed me to focus on key composers that we were studying at our orchestra field trip or one that I wanted to highlight because we were doing an activity using their music and have a second week where we could review that composer.

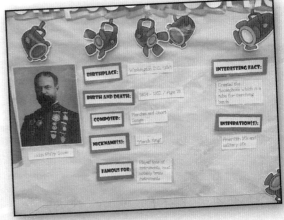

6

Keep it simple

Instead of reinventing the wheel, focusing on different facts and facets for every composer (and doing a ton of work to significantly change the board), I thought about what I really wanted my students to know. I decided on seven points that I wanted my students to be able to reference:

1. Birthplace
2. Birth and, where applicable, death dates
3. Type(s) of music composed
4. Nickname. Some composers had nicknames in life or were given one by a historian but if not, I make up one. It really helps everything stick.
5. Instrument(s) played. Limit this to the one or two they were famous for.
6. One interesting fact
7. Notable inspiration(s) for their pieces

Having a set approach not only gave focus to the board for my students, it made the process of creating the boards so much easier. I set my composer calendar at the beginning of the year, pull together all the fact, and have them waiting in a folder with the composers' pictures. During the year, I pull out the folder, staple the picture and facts onto the board under their respective label, and I'm done. So simple!

Add a map

Many of our children have no concept of where certain places are compared to where we live. To offer this perspective, I added a large laminated map above my board that we use to find the composer's country. I've also found it to be an incredibly handy reference to use with any grade when we sing a song from a different country.

Use it!

Just like I would plan any other lesson, I needed a plan to use the board.

Week One
1. Students walk into the music room while listening to a piece of music by that composer.
2. They sit down in front of the bulletin board and review the facts on the board.
3. I turn off the music and begin reviewing the facts on the board with students, adding fun facts to certain things as I see fit. I particularly like to give students a frame of reference for the time period during which the composer lived. For example: "Yes, this composer did live during the same time as George Washington."
4. We take no more than 5–7 minutes with the facts. Then, I turn on another piece of music by the composer. This is the signal for students to move quietly to their assigned seats so we can begin our next activity.

Week Two
1. Students walk into the music room while listening to a different (third) piece of music from the composer.
2. They walk to the board, choose one fact to put inside their brain, then move to their assigned seat.
3. We share (from our assigned seats) the facts about the composer, either with the entire class or with our shoulder partners.

ABraCaDaBra Assessments

Movement Challenge

Whenever possible, we repeat the music and movement a final time. During this time, I do not lead or participate in the movement. I tell my students that I will be watching to see who can hear when the music changes and who can't. When you are just observing and not worrying about moving, you can tell which children can hear it and which children are watching you or others for what to do. For more complicated movement patterns or those where a leader is needed, like those with parachute, this might not work. I have, however, had a few classes impress me with their ability to do the parachute by themselves while I record them for the website.

Lights, Camera, Action

If your students struggle without you as the example, record your students doing the activity and watch it later to assess. Making a video of a class that does a spectacular job is also a great way to make a huge deal of their effort. I'll ask students if I can record them, then I'll post the video, on my site or the school's, and send a note home to parents so they can check it out!

Of course you'll need to make sure that all students in the class have permission to have their photo taken. I'm fortunate that my school helps manage this, having parents sign a school-wide permission at the beginning of the year school. I keep a running list of those who *can't* have their photo taken and proceed accordingly.

MINT Paper

No, it is not a paper that smells like mint. MINT stands for Musician IN Thought. It is a short worksheet that asks what students thought the first time they heard a particular piece, what they imagine when they close their eyes and listen to it, and the one word they would use to describe it.

I will have students write a MINT paper after we've completed an activity with a strong listening component, playing the piece again as they are writing. I expect students to answer the first two questions with complete sentences, and to offer a one-word-only description for question three. I also include an "Additional comments" section for anything extra they might want to tell me about the piece or activity. A template is available at www.lorenz.com/resources/magical.

What's the Magic Word?

A simple written assessment, the Magic Word exit slip has blanks for today's magic word and its meaning. (Visit www.lorenz.com/resources/magical to download a template.) It's a great way to let parents know what their child is learning in music and a super quick way for you to see if the students got the concept.

Alternatively, if you are running low on time but still want to send something home, fill out the slip, give a copy to students as they leave your classroom to put in their folders, and tell them to share the "magic word" with their families.

You can also modify this assessment by providing the vocabulary word and having students fill out only the definition, or vice versa. The "magic word" can also be any concept that you're working on in class, be it from this resource or not.

Composer Corner Question and Answer

Extend the Composer Corner by keeping the board in place for a third week but hiding the answers. Give students a fill-in-the-blank worksheet or have them write down on dry erase boards as much information as they remember. Then, uncover each answer and see how much information they remembered. Visit www.lorenz.com/resources/magical to download a template and adapt it for your situation, filling in for students as much or as little information as you deem appropriate.

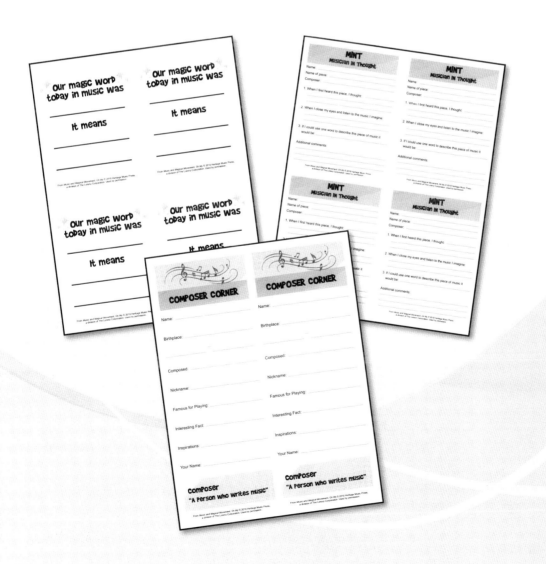

Kangaroo Expressions

Objectives

Students will aurally identify the difference between staccato and legato phrases.

Students will use movement to demonstrate the difference between staccato and legato.

Materials

Recording of "Kangaroos" from *The Carnival of the Animals* by Camille Saint-Saëns

Form Map

Form

A–B–A–B–A–B–Coda

Magic Words

Short and Long (K)
Staccato and Legato (1st)

This short and simple piece of music provides a great opportunity to explain short and long sounds to our young ones. Begin by discussing the vocabulary above that is appropriate for the grade level you are teaching. With my kindergarteners, I only use the vocabulary short sounds and long sounds. For my first graders, I venture into making the connection that short sounds are choppy and disconnected and long sounds tend to be more connected and smooth, and I begin using the words staccato and legato with them.

Then, ask your students to share some facts about kangaroos. Hopefully students will offer two main facts—that they jump, and that they have babies in their pouches. I usually add in the fact that those babies are called joeys.

Listen to "Kangaroos." During the music, demonstrate these motions:

A section *staccato sounds*	Keep your arms to your sides, bend at the elbow so your hands come up near your chest, and curve your hands (so your arms resemble a kangaroo's), and "jump" them to the rhythm of the music.
B section *legato sounds*	Put your hand to your forehead, "visor style" and move from side to side as if you're searching for something.
Coda *last arpeggiated chord*	Wrap your arms around your body like you're hugging yourself.

Ask students how many times you did each motion. (3 times for the A section, 3 times for the B section, and 1 hug at the end.) Explain what the motions mean: In the A section, the kangaroo is jumping around because it sounds staccato or has short sounds like jumping. In the B section the kangaroo is searching for a lost joey. At the end, the kangaroo found the joey and hugged him.

Listen to "Kangaroos" again and this time invite the children to do the motions with you while seated. To encourage participation, tell them that they will do bigger motions next, but you need to see who can do these smaller motions first.

For the third listen, students will find personal space and do these movements:

A section	Students jump to the rhythms in their personal space.
B section	Students crouch in a squatting position (like kangaroos rest) and look for the joey. It's a great workout for your lower body!
Coda *last arpeggiated chord*	Hug your joey because you are so happy you found him!

Extension Idea

You can always invite your students to create another movement to go along with the A and B sections. A student once told me that "Frogs jump too Mrs. Miller!" I took that connection, and during the A section we jumped like frogs and during the B section we sat on lilypads and caught flies with our tongues. It was very entertaining! If a student makes a connection, run with it.

Jumping Kangaroos (A section)

Where's the Joey? (B section)

Mrs. Miller's Magic Trick

Do your kiddos like to purposefully fall down during movement activities? Are they tempted to talk while music is playing? Mine are! Here are the expectations I give my class before this activity to help to prevent problems during the movement section:

1. This is not Bumper Kangaroos. Remember that you need to use your personal space wisely and be aware of who is around you.

2. Kangaroos are *expert* jumpers and they never fall while jumping so you shouldn't either.

3. In my classroom, when there is music playing, our mouths are silent. The music is doing the talking, not you. If you are talking while the music is talking you are being disrespectful, and being respectful is Mrs. Miller's number one rule.

Lion Long and Short

Objectives

Students will aurally identify the difference between long and short phrases.

Students will demonstrate the difference between long and short with movement.

Materials

Recording of "Introduction and Royal March of the Lion" from *The Carnival of the Animals* by Camille Saint-Saëns

Form map

Form

Introduction–A–B–A–Coda

Magic Words

Long and Short
Glissando

"Lion" uses two distinctively different sounds: There are the short, stately patterns during the A section and the glissando melody, which represents the roar of the lion, for the B section. I describe these sounds to my little ones as short (A section) and long (B section). Even though the piano is making a bunch of smaller sounds to create the ascending and descending pattern in the B section, it still creates a long sound to the ear.

Begin by discussing facts about lions with the class. Consider creating a diagram with the different facts. I settle on two facts that Saint-Saëns focused on in his composition: the lions' "king" status and their roar. (If you've recently done the Kangaroo Expressions lesson (see page 10), make a Venn Diagram comparing the "Introduction and Royal March of the Lion" and "Kangaroos.")

After the discussion, practice these movements:
- Stretch your paws and primp your mane.
- March to the steady beat in a very royal and regal manner, in personal space.
- Practice your biggest roar. During practice time this is an audible roar but it will become silent before you put it with the music. Practice a few times with an audible roar and then explain to students that "the music will be the roar so we need to keep our roar faces, but not let any sound come out of our mouths." Let students know there will be four roars in the music.
- Practice your best royal stance/pose.

Mrs. Miller's Magic Trick

When you are marching during a movement activity, remind students to have quiet feet. "We don't want to have a stomping ostinato during our piece of music." Practice this with students before the piece to ensure that the music will be the focus.

When you have practiced all of the movements, it's time to do the moves with the music!

Introduction	Stretch your paws and primp your mane
A section	March to the beat in a royal and regal manner
B section	Make your best lion roar face (4 times)
A section	March to the beat in a royal and regal manner
Coda	Strike a royal pose/stance

Since this piece is so short, you can easily do it twice. For variety, you can ask the girl lions to go first and ask the boy lions to watch and take notes on who did the best royal march or best roar face. Then, let the boys have a turn.

Extension Idea

If you are able to, bring out some instruments. Split the class in half (I use boy and girl lion groups) and have some play the steady beat with shaker instruments during the A section, then crescendo and decrescendo a shake on the ascending and descending roars in the B section.

Lion Long and Short

Introduction – A – B – A – Coda

Introduction – Primp yourself for a day in the jungle

A section – March around the jungle to see your kingdom

B section – Roar face to show the other animals that you are the king!

Coda – Show your best royal stand for your kingdom!

Glow in the Dark Fish

Objectives

Students will aurally identify contrasting themes in a piece of music.

Students will aurally identify different melodic directions in a piece of music.

Materials

Recording of "Aquarium" from *The Carnival of the Animals* by Camille Saint-Saëns

Scarves

Form map

Fluorescent juggling scarves (optional)

Blacklights (optional)

Form

A–B–A–B–A–C–Interlude–C–B–Coda

Magic Words

Theme
Ascending
Descending

Discuss what an aquarium is. What do fish in an aquarium have that fish in the ocean don't? What do fish in the ocean have that those in an aquarium don't? Explain to the children that you will be focusing on three different "fish moves"—one for each of the main sections of music.

A section	Swimming around and using our long, beautiful fins like angelfish
B section	Eating kelp from the top of the ocean all the way down to the ocean floor
C section	Freezing and hiding from the shark
Interlude	Swimming away to find a new hiding spot!
Coda	Swimming from the bottom of the ocean all the way to the surface and jumping out of the water!

 ## Mrs. Miller's Magic Trick

I share pictures of angelfish with my kiddos. We talk about how their fins are very flowy and delicate, and that their scarves should emulate these movements when they are swimming. This visual model helps keep them from just running around the room.

Be sure to encourage your children to use all levels when they are swimming during the A section. The B section is a wonderful example of a descending melody; make sure students stand on their tiptoes and start all the way at the top of the kelp and "munch" (squiggle the scarf) all the way down to the ground so that it matches the descending melody.

In the C section, when the glockenspiel plays, we put the scarves in front of our faces and freeze for the shark coming back. There is a short interlude between the repeat of the C section; we just swim to a new location and freeze another time for the shark.

The coda is an ascending line. As it begins, our fish swim really fast all the way from the bottom of the ocean to the top and then jump (throw the scarf) out of the ocean with a big flourish!

Extension Ideas

Use blacklights and fluorescent juggling scarves to add a little fun to this activity. I have 7 blacklights that I place in a big circle around my kiddos and then we do the same movements as above, but in the dark. I have also done this without the blacklights because I was short on time, and my kiddos never know the difference. You could also do this activity two weeks in row: the first week with no blacklights and the second week with them. Talk to the kids about the midnight zone of the ocean and how many creatures adapt to pitch black by glowing. Your fluorescent scarves represent those glowing fish.

Glow in the Dark Fish

A – B – A – B – A – C – Interlude – C – B – Coda

A section – Swim around showing off your beautiful angelfish fins!

B section – Eat some kelp. Start at the very top and go all the way to the bottom!

C section – Hide from the SHARK!

Coda – Swim all the way to the ocean's surface and ju

Sunshine and Thunder

Objectives

Students will aurally identify different themes in a piece of music.

Students will aurally identify high and low melodies in a piece of music.

Students will aurally identify accented (staccato) sounds and long (legato) sounds.

Materials

Recording of Rondo No. 11 from *30 Pieces for Children*, Op. 27 by Dmitry Kabalevsky

Recommended performer: Hiroshi Arimori on the album *Kabalevsky 2*

Pool noodles

Form map

Form

A–B–A'–B'–A–Coda

Magic Words

High and Low
Staccato and Legato (1st and 2nd)
Short and Long (K)

Discuss the characteristics of a thunderstorm. What is it like during a storm? Try to pull words like "loud" or "dark" from the students so you can use those words to describe the music later. Then discuss what it is like when the storm ends. Sunshine? Perhaps a rainbow? During this discussion, guide the children toward words like "light" and "soft" so that you can use these words to describe the music too.

Explain that this song has light and dark sounds in it. During the A sections we imagine a thunderstorm and in the B sections students will imagine sunshine and a rainbow after the storm. The Coda includes snippets of both the A and B materials, so we alternate between Thunder and Sunshine movements.

Demonstrate a movement that pantomimes a thunderstorm. For example, you could stomp your feet for thunder and slide your hands for lightning. Then pantomime sunshine, perhaps by putting your arms up like a rainbow and walking on soft feet that are like fluffy clouds.

Listen to the song as the children pantomime movements for each section. Remind students that you are looking for friends that get to earn the pool noodles for movement.

Have students sit on the floor in personal space. Demonstrate the following three movements with pool noodles:

Thunder	Pounding the pool noodle on the ground. Make sure you show students that the pool noodle should not bend a lot when you pound it or it won't make the sound.
Lightning	I like to harness my inner Zeus during this time and think of how he would throw his lightning bolts. No one should actually throw their pool noodles though, nor should they touch other people's lightning bolts.
Sunshine/Rainbow	Hold on to both ends of the pool noodle and bend it slightly over your head and rock back and forth. Some smaller kids might not be able to reach both ends. They they can hold the middle and one end to bend the noodle into a rainbow.

Give a pool noodle to each child. Practice each movement as a group a few times. Then play the music and perform as a class with the pool noodles. Students will use a combination of the thunder and lightning moves during the A section (The Angry Storm!). Remind them that storms have both so they might want to do one or the other or both! It is their creative decision to make. This piece is short so we usually get to perform it more than one time!

Mrs. Miller's Magic Trick

If you have bigger classes, you can split them into two groups to make this activity work better, giving one group the pool noodles while the other group pantomimes the movements. Switch groups and listen to the song again.

Sunshine and Thunder

A – B – A' – B' – A – Coda

A section – The Angry Storm!
B section – The Sunshine and Rainbows
Coda – The Storm and Sunshine go back and forth!

Low and Slow Elephants

Objectives

Students will use movement to show the adagio tempo of a piece of music.

Students will use movement to show the ABA form of a piece of music.

Materials

Recording of "The Elephant" from *The Carnival of the Animals* by Camille Saint-Saëns

Parachute

Form map

Form

A–B–A

Magic Words

Tempo
Adagio
Form

Before teaching this lesson, I make sure my students have heard various examples of slow and fast music and have experienced some slow movements and fast movements with that music. You will also want to have some rules in place for parachute fun.

 ## Mrs. Miller's Magic Trick

Rules for Parachute Fun

1. Anytime there is music playing, our mouths are closed so we can focus our ears on the music.

2. When we hold the parachute our knuckles should be showing, not our thumbs. This way students won't hurt their wrists while holding the parachute up.

3. If you are too rough (not safe) with the parachute, you will have to leave the parachute.

Have a class discussion on the characteristics of an elephant. Write some facts the students offer on the board.

Low and Slow Elephants

A – B – A

A section – Trunks move slowly back and forth to the steady beat

B section – Clean up time! Go to the pond and wash off!

Don't forget to give a big Elephant trumpet at the very end!

Discuss the ABA form of the piece with the students. Make sure they understand that ABA means same-different-same. Then practice these moves with them:

A section	Students will pretend that their arms are the trunk of the elephant and they will move their trunk from side to side (moving the parachute left to right). Remind them that the elephant's trunk moves slowly, so they should move slowly. Also remind students that their feet should be planted on the floor during this time.
B section	Boys will lift up the parachute over their heads and girls will go under the parachute into the "pool of water." They will pretend to be elephants taking a bath and getting some water. Halfway through the B section, have girl elephants come back and call the boy elephants to the pool to take their baths.
A section	Return to swinging "trunks". At the end of the last A section we all raise our trunks and then wave at each other under the parachute.

If time allows, I get my kiddos to pantomime the motions with a pretend parachute first with the music and then pull out the real thing. This is a great behavior management tool because you can remind the kiddos that you are looking for friends that can follow directions to use the real thing!

Extension Ideas
If you want to change things up with the movements and do this activity another way, try these movements instead:

A section	Walk slowly around the circle, holding the parachute with one hand and swinging the other hand like a trunk.
B section	Hold the parachute over heads while girl elephants slowly trade places with another girl elephant. Then boy elephants will do the same.

You could also have a class discussion and invite students to suggest different slow movements you could do to represent the elephant.

Mrs. Miller's Magic Trick

You'll often hear elephant sounds during the B section. As long as they aren't too loud (and they usually aren't) I let this slide since they are really using those imaginations.

Mirror Flags

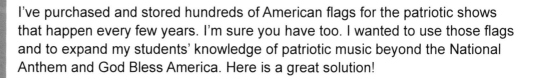

Objectives

Students will identify characteristics of patriotic music.

Students will identify characteristics of a march.

Students will demonstrate their understanding of steady beat through movement.

Materials

Recording of "Washington Post March" by John Philip Sousa

American flags, 2 per student

Form map

Form

Introduction–AA–BB–CC–DCDC

Mrs. Miller's Magic Trick

This is a great opportunity to discuss the significance of the flag. We talk about how we should not allow a flag to touch the ground, and the respect we should have for a national symbol (even though ours is made of plastic).

Magic Words

March
Band
Sousa

I've purchased and stored hundreds of American flags for the patriotic shows that happen every few years. I'm sure you have too. I wanted to use those flags and to expand my students' knowledge of patriotic music beyond the National Anthem and God Bless America. Here is a great solution!

Discuss the style of marches and John Philip Sousa with your class. The week I teach this lesson, Sousa is on my composer corner bulletin board and we discuss facts about Sousa and the significance that marches had in American history.

Next, discuss what a mirror image is. I do some physical warm-up movements with my kiddos to practice what mirroring should look like with a partner.

Review with students the form of the "Washington Post March." Discuss how many times we will be leaders and followers, and also how many times students will follow the teacher.

Have students choose a partner and pass out American flags. Each student needs two flags. Have them find personal space facing their partners.

Students must determine who will be Partner A and who will be Partner B. I usually do this by height. For example, the tallest partner is Partner A and the shortest is Partner B.

Make sure no student has their back completely to you. When we get to the C section, they will need to turn and face the teacher; that should take only a quarter turn.

Display the form using the provided visual or by writing it on the board. Guide students through these movements:

Introduction *14 beats*	Stand still, arms at sides, heads bowed
A section *24 beats*	Mirror Partner A

A section *24 beats*	Mirror Partner A
B section *24 beats*	Mirror Partner B
B section *24 beats*	Mirror Partner B
C section *24 beats*	Mirror Teacher
C section *24 beats*	Mirror Teacher
D section *16 beats*	Beat 1, Left Flag up at diagonal* Beat 5, Right Flag up at diagonal Beat 9, Both Flags up
C section *24 beats*	Improvise steady beat moves
D section *16 beats*	Beat 1, Left Flag up at diagonal Beat 5, Right Flag up at diagonal Beat 9, Both Flags up
C section *24 beats*	March in personal space
Last beat	Freeze in a patriotic pose!

*The flag "hits" in the D section correspond to the accents in the low brass and bass drum.

Extension Ideas

Encourage pairs to work together to create their own choreography for the A, B, and C sections. Listen to the piece as a class and have students jot down ideas or brainstorm together. Listen again so students can set eight-beat movements for each eight-beat phrase. They will need to come up with nine in all (three for each section). Keep the introduction and DCDC section from the original. See how creative your kiddos can get!

Many marches have the same form as "Washington Post March," so many that the form is called March Form. Band geeks or those using this with older students who have had some band exposure may want to use this to introduce the special names used for sections in marches: A section = First strain; B section = Second strain; C section = Trio; and D section = Break strain.

Brass Boulevard

Objectives

Students will identify instruments in the Brass family.

Students will identify aural characteristics of instruments in the Brass family.

Materials

Recording of "Toreador Song" from *Carmen* by Georges Bizet

Recommended performers: Empire Brass

Parachute

Form Map

Brass Family visuals

Form

A–A–B–C–A–Interlude–D–A–Coda

Magic Words

Brass Family
Form

Use the Brass Characteristics visual to present the characteristics of the brass family. You will focus on three characteristics of all brass instruments: detachable mouthpiece; made of brass; and flared horn (or bell).

Discuss the timbre that brass instruments have. You can use the words bright and present to describe the timbre. Explain that the brass players sit in the back of the orchestra because of their timbre.

Discuss the form of "Toreador Song" with the class. There is no introduction and the A section reigns supreme—it keeps coming back again and again!

🎩 Mrs. Miller's Magic Trick

When you use a parachute, always pantomime the movements with the music first. The parachute is a very exciting manipulative and no matter how many times you say it, it is very hard for students to quiet themselves when they get started with the parachute. You want them to have one full listen to the music without the excitement of the parachute.

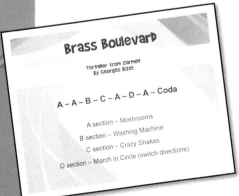

Brass Boulevard

Toreador from Carmen
By Georges Bizet

A – A – B – C – A – D – A – Coda

A section – Mushrooms
B section – Washing Machine
C section – Crazy Shakes
D section – March in Circle (switch directions)

Made of Brass

Brass Family Characteristics

Here are the movements for each section (with thanks to my aunt Artie Almeida for some of the terminology):

A section *32 beats*	**Mushroom x4** The children will slowly raise the parachute on the accented first beat of each eight-beat phrase and let it fall down on its own.
A section *32 beats*	**Mushroom x4**
B section *16 beats*	**Washing Machine** Students move their arms from left to right to create a swirling effect in the parachute like the movement you see in a washing machine. Sometimes you just get big waves, and that's fine too.
C section *20 beats*	**Crazy Shakes** Shake the parachute to no particular beat. I encourage kids to start the crazy shakes small and get bigger to match the crescendo in this section.
A section *32 beats*	**Mushroom x4**
Interlude *8 beats*	Students turn to their right, let go of the parachute with their right hand, and stand still.
D section *92 beats*	Students march for 12 measures (48 beats) while the French horn plays the melody. When the melody moves to the trumpet, students switch hands on the parachute and turn, and march in the opposite direction.
A section *32 beats*	**Mushroom x4**
Coda	**Ceiling Stick** Count down "3, 2, 1, GO!" On GO! everyone will lift the parachute and let go. The parachute should stick to the ceiling. It's very fun when it works, however it may not work every time, particularly if your ceiling is high or is not flat.

 Mrs. Miller's Magic Trick

To get the parachute to stick to the ceiling, it is crucial that everyone lets go at the same time! If my kiddos don't get it right the first time I usually just let them try to stick it one more time. I also make sure that no one moves when the parachute is up in the air because when it comes down, you don't want kids rushing to try and get under it... someone could get hurt!

Woodwind Way

Objectives

Students will identify instruments in the Woodwind family.

Students will identify aural characteristics of instruments in the Woodwind family.

Materials

Recording of *Kleine Kammermusik*, Op. 24, No. 2, movement IV, "Schnelle Viertel" by Paul Hindemith

Suggested performer: Swiss Woodwind Quintet

Ribbon streamers

Form map

Woodwind Family visuals

Form

Rondo (A–B–A–C–A–D–A–E–A–F–A)

Mrs. Miller's Magic Trick

Don't forget to announce each solo instrument while the students listen to the solo sections!

Magic Words

Woodwind Family
Form
Solo or Ensemble
Quintet

Demonstrate the characteristics of the woodwind family, using the downloadable visuals if you wish (see page 2). Focus on the characteristics that are usually found in woodwind instruments: they're made of wood, or were at one time (except for the saxophone); most of them have a reed; and they have many keys.

Discuss the timbre of woodwind instruments. They tend to have warm tones in the lower range and bright tones in the higher range.

This piece is in rondo form. Talk about rondo with your students. Let them know that each time they hear the A section, they will hear the entire quintet. During each of the other sections, they will hear one instrument playing a solo. This is a great way for students to hear each of the instruments individually and quickly. They will also hear one instrument that is not in the woodwind family: the French horn.

Mrs. Miller's Magic Trick

The French horn became a member of the woodwind quintet because composers noticed that its mellow tones blend well with the woodwind instruments and they started including it in their woodwind quintets.

A section	Students will move their ribbon streamers freely to match the pitch played by each instrument. I ask that students not move their feet so that they can maintain their personal space and keep their ribbon streamers from getting tangled with others'.
All other sections	Students will freeze in a pose. I have a rule that all students must keep both feet on the floor. Otherwise, kiddos will be falling all over the place because they are trying to balance on one foot.

Extension Idea

After students have performed it once, switch the moves: have students freeze during the A sections and move their streamers freely during the other sections.

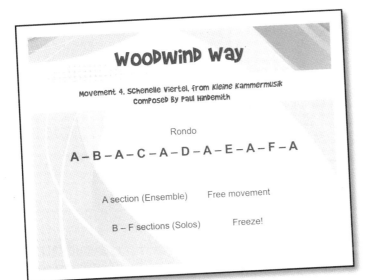

WOODWIND WAY

Movement 4, Schenelle Viertel, from Kleine Kammermusik
Composed By Paul Hindemith

Rondo

A – B – A – C – A – D – A – E – A – F – A

A section (Ensemble)   Free movement

B – F sections (Solos)   Freeze!

Woodwind Family Characteristics

out of wood

Exception is the saxophone.

Most are played by small piece of wood reed, against a mout

Exceptions are the flute and piccolo.

Percussion Place

Moves created by Christina Torrez, a very talented music teacher, who gave me permission to share this great movement activity!

Objectives

Students will identify instruments in the Percussion family.

Students will identify aural characteristics of instruments in the Percussion family.

Materials

Recording of "Log Cabin Blues" by George Hamilton

Recommended performer: Eastman Marimba Band though it can be hard to find. A good substitute is O-Zone Percussion Group and Gary Olmstead, who play this piece on their album *Whiplash*.

Scarves, 2 per student

Form map

Percussion Family visuals

Form

Introduction–A–A–B–B–A–C–C–D–D–D–Coda

Magic Words

Percussion Family
Form

Demonstrate the characteristics of the percussion family. Focus on the one main characteristic that all percussion instruments have in common: you hit, shake, or scrape them to play. Use the provided visuals if you wish.

Discuss the timbre of the percussion family. There are hundreds of instruments in the percussion family, and therefore hundreds of different timbres. In general, though, they are usually pretty loud and therefore the percussion section is always at the very back of the orchestra.

Talk about the form of "Log Cabin Blues." I usually point out the D section is repeated three times—this is very unusual. The B or A section is normally the one that is repeated the most.

Ask, "Do you hear more than five instruments? More than ten? More than fifteen?" There's not a score in print so there's not a "right" answer. What's important is making sure your students recognize that they are hearing many instruments.

Here are the moves for each section (with thanks to my aunt Artie Almeida who invented some of the terminology):

Introduction *8 beats*	Stand still with scarves
A section *32 beats*	**Friendly Faces** Walk around to the music with a bounce in your step while moving your scarves next to your body. Smile at others as you pass them. At the end of this A section, have students freeze to transition to the next A section.
A section *32 beats*	**Friendly Faces** (without the freeze at the end)

B section *32 beats*	**Criss Cross Circles** Both scarves cross in front of your body and go up into a big circle over 4 beats. Repeat 3 times for 12 beats. Then, students freeze in a fun pose for 4 beats. Do 4 more big circles (12 beats) and a 4-beat freeze. (In this first B section the bird whistle has the melody.)
B section *32 beats*	**Criss Cross Circles**
A section *32 beats*	**Friendly Faces**
C section *24 beats*	**Shoulder Dance** Make a fist around the scarf, with one in each hand. Then bend your knees and plant your heels and move your toes from side to side, moving the scarves over your shoulders. (The flapper dances of the 1920s are the inspiration for this move.) Freeze at the end of this section.
C section *24 beats*	**Shoulder Dance**
D section *24 beats*	**Cheerleader Dance** Beat 1: Right hand up Beat 2: Left hand up Beat 3: Right hand to the right Beat 4: Left hand to the left Beats 5–6: Toss scarves up Beats 7–8: Catch scarves Beat 9: Stomp one foot Beat 10: Stomp the other foot Beats 11–12: Pat lap twice Beats 13–14: Bump fists twice Beats 15–16: Bring one arm up on each beat Beats 17–20: Bring hands around in a circle Beats 21–22: Toss scarves up Beats 23–24: Catch scarves
D section *24 beats*	**Cheerleader Dance**
D section *24 beats*	**Cheerleader Dance**
Coda *8 beats*	**Squiggle Scarf** Squiggle your scarves all the way down to the floor and then throw them up in the air when you hear the accent in the music.

Mrs. Miller's Magic Trick

You are going to burn some *major* calories with this movement activity! Don't be afraid to get into the music with your kiddos. Really move your body and swing those scarves while you walk to emulate the feeling of "Log Cabin Blues". And that shoulder dance? Do it like you mean it so that your kids are not afraid to try it!

Extension Idea

Match each student to an unpitched percussion instrument in the classroom. You can assign them or give students one minute to walk around the room and select one. Each student then completes an information sheet about their instrument and presents their instrument to the class. Your info page can include anything from how it's played to a description of its timbre.

Strings Street

Objectives

Students will identify instruments in the String family.

Students will identify aural characteristics of instruments in the String family.

Materials

Recording of "Allegretto" from *Palladio* by Karl Jenkins

Scarves

Ribbon streamers

An approximately 1'x4' strip of fabric or other small divider that can be placed on the floor

Form map

String Family visuals

Form

Introduction–A–B–A–C–Interlude–C–Interlude–D–A–B–A–Coda

MrS. Miller's MAGiC Trick

Using stories is a great way to help students get into the music. For this lesson, I always dress up in a robe and have a wand. Do as much "acting" as you see fit!

Magic Words

String Family
Form

Demonstrate the characteristics of the string family, focusing on the most important characteristic that all string instruments have in common: they all have strings! A few supporting visuals are provided at www.lorenz.com/resources/magical if you want to use them.

Discuss the timbre of string instruments. String instruments are used at many different dynamic levels, but they can be easily drowned out by other instruments so they are always at the front of the orchestra.

Talk about the form of *Allegretto*. It has some patterns in it and it has an interlude. Be sure to discuss with your students what an interlude is. I describe it as a short section that connects two other sections to help make a smoother transition.

Begin with the backstory: We will divide the class into two houses—House of Rallentando and House of Moderato. Rallentando students have streamer wands and Moderato students have scarf wands. They are practicing their spells in their own houses for a pretend battle that they will have in spells class this week.

Divide the class evenly however you want. If you have enough time, you can do the song twice so that students have a chance to be in both houses.

Demonstrate the movements for each house before you hand out their supplies. Put a strip of fabric or other divider in the center of your space (dividing it horizontally if you can). The groups should face each other. Remind House of Rallentando that they should never move their feet since they have streamers.

Introduction 8 beats	Stand still with scarves.
A section 32 beats	**Moderatos** tiptoe with scarves at their faces, creeping around in the shadows to find someone to put a spell on.
B section 32 beats	**Rallentandos** improvise spell moves with their ribbon streamers. Encourage them to make their spell moves follow the rhythmic changes in the piece.

A section *32 beats*	**Moderatos** repeat the first A section.
C section *28 beats*	**Moderatos** hold their scarves with both hands, moving the scarves around their bodies to create a force field that protects them from other spells. Their feet aren't moving, but they are moving their force fields all over their bodies. (Point out to your students that the soloist during this section is a violist!)
Interlude *4 beats*	**Moderatos** freeze where they are because they think they hear someone coming!
C section *28 beats*	**Moderatos** repeat the first C section. (This time the solo is played by a violin.)
Interlude *4 beats*	**Moderatos** freeze where they are because they think they hear someone coming!
D section *32 beats*	**Rallentandos** practice the X's and O's spell. Use your streamers to draw 2 X's in the air followed by 4 O's in the air right after it. Each X will take 2 beats to create. Each O will be done in 1 beat. This 8-beat pattern of 2 X's and 4 O's will be done 4 times, each in a different location: First 8 beats – in front of you Second 8 beats – on the right side Third 8 beats – on the left side Fourth 8 beats – above your head
A section *32 beats*	**Moderatos** repeat the first A section.
B section *32 beats*	**Rallentandos** repeat the first B section.
A section *32 beats*	**Moderatos** repeat the first A section
Coda *28 beats*	**Moderatos and Rallentandos:** Both houses are up at the final battle! Rallentando is casting spells and Moderato is blocking spells and casting their own! Everyone must stay in their own house (on their own side of the divider) and their wand may not cross that divider. At the very end, everyone can put their wands down or up into the air to show that the battle is over.

Mrs. Miller's Magic Trick

Your leading of both parts is the key to this activity working correctly. Near the end of each section, make sure to work your way back to the middle so you're in position to demonstrate what is coming up next. Practice on your own first so you have it down; then, do it with your students.

Mrs. Miller's Magic Trick

While the Moderatos are doing their moves, the Rallentandos must be crouching on the ground waiting for their turns, and vice versa. I tell students that they may not play with their "wands" during this time because it is a distraction. You can decide how strict you want to be with this point.

Extension Idea

Have your students create a different back story or perhaps help you decide on new moves for each section to create new spells.

Character collage

Objectives

Students will aurally identify and demonstrate through movement the sections of a theme and variation form.

Students will use movement to demonstrate orchestral timbres and dynamics.

Materials

Recording of the "Rakes of Mallow" from the *Irish Suite* by Leroy Anderson

Scarves

Form map

Form

Introduction—Theme (AB) and Variations (AB′ AB″ AB‴ AB‴′)—Coda

Magic Words

Percussion Family
Form

Scatter the children around the room, making sure they each have plenty of personal space.

Discuss the meaning of "Rakes of Mallow." Rakes are men that have no morals and make poor decisions in their lives. Mallow is a town in County Cork, Ireland. I skip the no morals and specific geography and just tell my students that this piece was written to describe men from the town of Mallow. It was written in 1780 and is now used as Notre Dame's fight song.

Talk about what theme and variations means. Explain how there is a theme and four variations in "Rakes of Mallow," as well as an introduction and a coda.

Here are the movements for each section. Unless noted, the A and B sections are always 32 beats each.

Introduction *16 beats*	Hold a scarf in front of your face like you're hiding. Move it side to side with the accents of the music.
Theme Children	A: Dance and skip with your scarf. B: Jump on beat 1 and throw the scarf in the air three times. Then wiggle the scarf down to the ground.
Variation 1 Gazelles	A: Prance with your scarf as reins (hold the scarf stretched between both hands). B: Leap with a flourish of your scarf on each beat 1.
Variation 2 Soldiers	A: Use the scarf as a scepter and become a solider. March around the room to the steady beat. B: Salute to your fellow soldiers three times. At the beginning of the fourth measure, bow to your fellow soldiers. You will recognize that the salutes and bows will follow the melody of the music.

Variation 3 Superheroes	A: Turn the scarves into capes! Fly around to save the day. B: Show off your muscles and your winning grin! Wave to your adoring fans!
Variation 4 Conductors *The tempo is the same but the meter changes in this variation*	A: Conduct the orchestra with your batons (scarves). Make sure to make gestures for louder or softer, and to bring certain instruments in and out, etc. A repeated: Continue as above B: Faster conducting! Try to keep up!
Coda	Fall on the floor, exhausted!

 ## Mrs. Miller's Magic Trick

Practice the motions without music, then turn on the recording and perform with your students. The more you are in character, the more they will be! Have fun with it.

Extension Ideas

Have students choose a different character to represent each variation. They should be able to justify their character choices using appropriate music vocabulary.

Play other examples of theme and variations. One of my favorites is the *Russian Sailors Dance* by Glière.

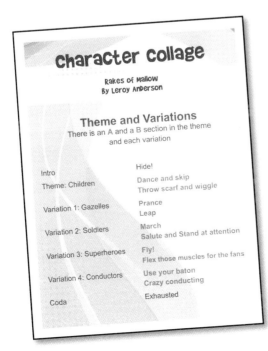

Character Collage

Rakes of Mallow
By Leroy Anderson

Theme and Variations
There is an A and a B section in the theme
and each variation

Intro	Hide!
Theme: Children	Dance and skip Throw scarf and wiggle
Variation 1: Gazelles	Prance Leap
Variation 2: Soldiers	March Salute and Stand at attention
Variation 3: Superheroes	Fly! Flex those muscles for the fans
Variation 4: Conductors	Use your baton Crazy conducting
Coda	Exhausted

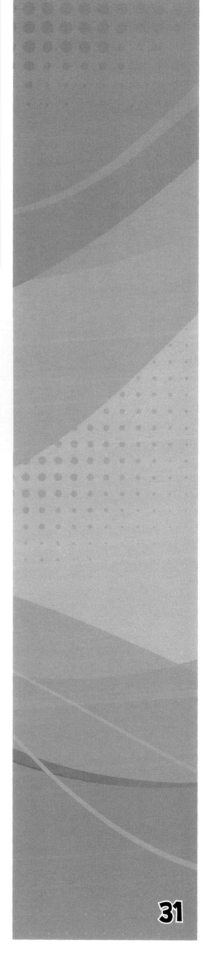

Sailors' Variations

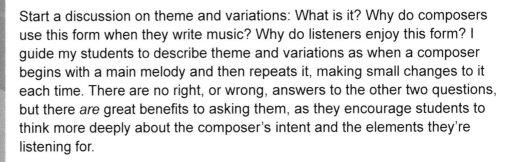

Objectives

Students will aurally identify and demonstrate through movement the sections of a theme and variation form.

Materials

Recording of "Russian Sailors Dance" by Reinhold Glière

Parachute

Form map

Form

Theme and Variations

Mrs. Miller's Magic Trick

Open-ended questions are great for listening activities because they help the students to broaden their minds and to listen for and understand all the qualities of the music.

Magic Words

Theme and variations
Tempo
Dynamics

Start a discussion on theme and variations: What is it? Why do composers use this form when they write music? Why do listeners enjoy this form? I guide my students to describe theme and variations as when a composer begins with a main melody and then repeats it, making small changes to it each time. There are no right, or wrong, answers to the other two questions, but there *are* great benefits to asking them, as they encourage students to think more deeply about the composer's intent and the elements they're listening for.

Begin by introducing each of these movements without the parachute:

Mushroom	Slowly lift the parachute and let it fall on its own, creating a mushroom shape.
Quick Mushroom	Lift the parachute quickly over 4 beats and pull it down quickly over 4.
Washing Machine	Everyone moves only their arms left to right, which creates an agitation effect like an old washing machine.
Small Shakes	Students move their hands up and down in small motions very quickly to make ripples in the parachute. In these activity, small shakes are done at stomach level and overhead.
Big Shakes	Students make a larger movement up and down, creating big waves in the parachute.

Next, pantomime the movements on pages 34–35 to the music, making sure that everyone is doing them correctly and safely.

Finally, perform with the parachute, and repeat if time allows. As students are lining up to leave, ask questions about how the movements complemented each variation.

Extension Ideas

Notice that each variation also features one of the orchestra families! You could go over this piece again and, instead of focusing on the theme and variations, discuss the orchestra families and their distinct timbres.

Divide the class into eight groups, providing each with a different prop (scarves, streamers, stretchy bands, small parachutes, etc.). Assign each group a variation and have them create a new movement sequence for it. (You're in charge of the introduction and coda to bring all the groups together at the beginning and end.) Perform the student-created sequence.

Here are the movements for each section. Each variation is 24 beats (with one exception as listed below), however the tempo does change with most of the variations.

Introduction (*28 beats*) *quick and anticipatory*	Stand still. Use facial expressions to get the children excited about what will happen next.
Theme (*48 beats*) *low notes, largo*	**Mushroom** Lift up the parachute slowly on beat 1 and let it fall down on its own. You dictate when to lift it again (ideally on a beat 1).
Variation 1 (*24 beats*) *tambourine, higher notes*	**Small Shakes** Hold the parachute at stomach level and move hands up and down in small motions very quickly to make ripples in the parachute.
Variation 2 (*24 beats*) *highest notes, flute*	**Small Shakes** Repeat small shakes, but have the students shake above their heads so that the parachute is above them. (I pull my side of the parachute tight so that it stays up.)
Variation 3 (*24 beats*) *moderato, brass family*	**March** to the steady beat in a circle to the right, holding the parachute with one hand.
Variation 4 (*24 beats*) *adagio, continue brass*	Switch hands on the parachute. **March** at half tempo in a circle to the left.
Variation 5 (*24 beats*) *mezzo piano, woodwind family,* *pizzicato strings*	Slowly lay the **parachute on the ground**.
Variation 6 (*24 beats*) *presto, string family*	Students bend their knees and **pat the steady beat** on their laps.
Variation 7 (*24 beats*) *allegro, strong melody*	**Washing Machine** Pick up the parachute and move arms left to right.

Variation 8 *(48 beats)* *forte, percussion*	**Big Shakes** Students move their hands up and down to the steady beat creating big waves in the parachute. The kids will probably get a little excited here.
Coda *orchestra to the max!*	**Quick Mushroom x4** *(32 beats)* Pull the parachute up for four beats and then pull it down for four beats. **Small Shakes** *(24 beats)* As soon as you reach the bottom of the last mushroom start Small Shakes. Count down "4, 3, 2, GO!" during the last 4 beats. **Ceiling stick** Students release on the next downbeat, throwing the parachute up to the ceiling. If everyone releases at the same time, the parachute will stick to the ceiling for a few seconds. (If you do not have a short or flat ceiling you can still have the students throw the parachute. But instead of letting go yourself, pull it back quickly to grab the whole thing. You will definitely see some smiles!)

Storm Story

Objectives

Students will identify the characteristics of program music.

Students will create movement to complement a particular theme.

Materials

Recording of Symphony No. 6, Fourth Movement (Allegro) by Ludwig van Beethoven

Scarves, 1 or 2 per student

Form map

Form

Free Form

This activity can be done as an individual movement activity or a group one. Use the approach that is best for your kiddos and classroom set-up.

Magic Words

Program music
Locomotor and Non-locomotor movement
Free form

Discuss with the class the characteristics of a thunderstorm. What are some things that might happen during a thunderstorm? (rain, thunder, hail, etc.)

Talk about patterns with students and about how some composers like to stick to a pattern and use repeated sections, and some composers want to tell a story with their music and might not repeat anything. We call this program music. This music doesn't have a specific form.

Give each student a scarf and show them a few examples of 4- or 8-beat movements that demonstrate a part of a storm. For lightning, for example, I hold the scarf tight vertically in my hands for 4 beats, then let go with the top hand to let the scarf whip forward towards the ground for 4 beats. Tell students that you will announce a part of a storm (thunder, lightning, etc.) and they will create their own movements.

After they've warmed up with some ideas, give students any movement parameters (i.e. locomotor vs. non-locomotor) and the five parts of the thunderstorm: Thunder, Lightning, Rain, Hail, and Wind. Students will work independently for a few minutes to set their movements for each part of the storm. To do this as a group movement activity, divide the class into five groups, giving each group one of the parts of the storm.

There are three sections where everyone will do the same things. Here are those movements, along with an outline of the other sections:

Calm before the storm *0:00–0:27*	Everyone starts from a seated position. Students slowly stand and prepare their scarves for the thunder. Do this part dramatically as if the storm is rising up out of the ground. For group performances, have each group sit together and move their scarves along the ground to be the "rumbling of the storm." Then, call the groups in the timed order that follows. Each group will stand to do its movement for the class and then sit when their turn is over.

Thunder *(0:27–0:49)* **Lightning** *(0:49–1:11)* **Rain** *(1:11–1:35)* **Hail** *(1:35–1:56)* **Wind** *(1:56–2:26)*	Students perform their movements (individually or in groups) for each of the storm movements.
All storm events 2:26–2:49	Student put together their thunder, lightning, rain, hail, and wind movements. In group performances, all groups will stand and perform their movements.
Storm fades away 2:49–3:21	Students continue putting together all of their storm movements but gradually make them smaller and smaller until they are sitting on the floor again, just like we began, with the scarf balled up in their fists.
Flowers bloom 3:21–end	As this part begins, students will open their fists very slowly, allowing the scarf to "bloom" out of their hands and expand, like a flower blooming.

Extension Idea

This great movement activity that really tells a story is an excellent way to showcase what is going on in your classroom to your parents, community, and school administration. Consider recording a class doing their movements and telling the story, then post it to the school website!

Storm Story

Beethoven's Symphony No. 6, Mvt. 4, "Allegro"

Free Form
Various motif are placed throughout the piece
Programmatic music—the music is telling a story
Each instrument represents something

Calm before the storm
Thunder
Lightning
Rain
Hail
Wind
All
Storm fades away
Flowers bloom

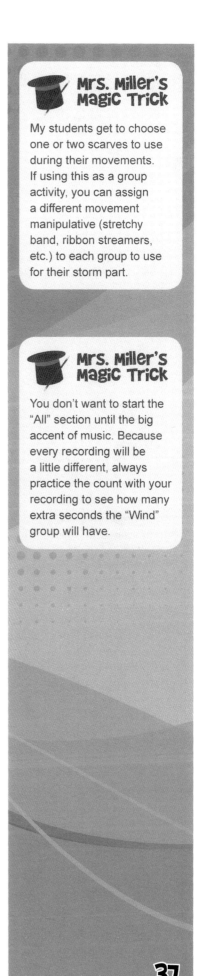

Mrs. Miller's Magic Trick

My students get to choose one or two scarves to use during their movements. If using this as a group activity, you can assign a different movement manipulative (stretchy band, ribbon streamers, etc.) to each group to use for their storm part.

Mrs. Miller's Magic Trick

You don't want to start the "All" section until the big accent of music. Because every recording will be a little different, always practice the count with your recording to see how many extra seconds the "Wind" group will have.

Olympic Achievements

Objectives

Students will create movements to match a theme or lyrics.

Students will be able to identify why a piece of music is used for various events/purposes (e.g. Olympics, advertising, 4th of July).

Students will identify why a theme is important to a piece of music.

Materials

Recordings of "Bugler's Dream" by Leo Arnaud and "Olympic Theme and Fanfare" by John Williams

Recommended performers: Cleveland Symphonic Winds, Frederick Fennell conductor

Various manipulatives (parachute, super stretchy, bouncy balls, scarves, ribbon scarves, etc.)

Winter or Summer Olympics visuals (print and laminate)

Form

Class-created rondo

Magic Words

Movement
Theme
Melody

Every two years a summer or winter Olympics is plastered all over our TVs and social media feeds, and with it comes the seemingly endless airing of the Olympic theme. Because students will hear this piece over and over again, they should be able to put a name to it and understand why it is called a theme.

🎩 Mrs. Miller's Magic Trick

The Olympic Theme known to most Americans, courtesy of NBC, is actually a medley of two themes: Leo Arnaud's "Bugler's Dream" and John Williams's "Olympic Theme and Fanfare." The Smithsonian.com article "Who Really Composed NBC's Olympic Theme? Not Who You Think" does a great job telling this interesting tale.

Play "Bugler's Dream" for your students, starting after the timpani introduction, and see if they can identify what it is used for. Play it again, fitting the lyrics below to the familiar theme. Use the "winter" or "summer" version depending on which Olympics are closest. This theme will become the A section for a rondo you'll create with the students.

Winter Olympics
PyeongChang, Korea hosts the
Winter Olympics in Twenty Eighteen
What sport are you in charge of?
Come on please tell us for all the world to hear

Summer Olympics
Tokyo, a city in Japan hosts the
Games in Twenty Twenty
What sport are you in charge of?
Come on please tell us for all the world to hear

Mrs. Miller's Magic Trick

I make singing the poem optional. While singing it gives them bonus points with me, they can use their speaking voices and say it in rhythm. The lyrics for 2018 and 2020 are listed here. Follow their form to create new lyrics for other years and sites.

Once students have learned the main refrain, break them into four groups. Give each group a printed copy of one of the four Olympic-event poems. For Winter, the poems are about figure skating, bobsleigh, ski jump, and snowboarding. For summer, they're gymnastics, track and field, swimming, and ball-and-court sports (like tennis and basketball). Each group will also need a movement prop. You may choose which prop goes with which movement or let each group select
its prop.

Listen to the theme from John Williams's "Olympic Theme and Fanfare." (Many recordings of "Olympic Theme" are a mash up of Arnaud's fanfare and Williams's theme, in which case this will be the B section.) Speak one of the event poems to this melody and rhythm. After your demonstration, give each group about two minutes to fit their poem to this music.

After they've learned the poem, each group should create at least one movement for each phrase of the poem. Students can develop more specific movements if they choose; at minimum, however, they'll need to create four separate movements (one for each of the four phrases).

To perform, alternate singing Arnaud's theme with a performance by each small group of its poem and movements.

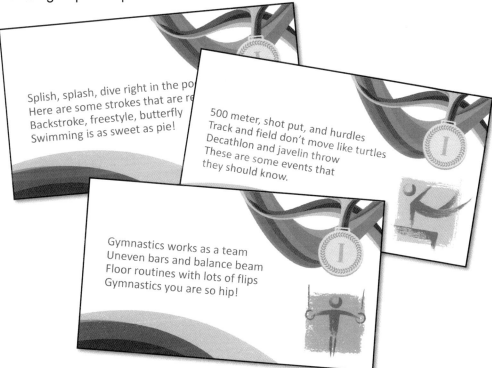

Splish, splash, dive right in the po
Here are some strokes that are r
Backstroke, freestyle, butterfly
Swimming is as sweet as pie!

500 meter, shot put, and hurdles
Track and field don't move like turtles
Decathlon and javelin throw
These are some events that
they should know.

Gymnastics works as a team
Uneven bars and balance beam
Floor routines with lots of flips
Gymnastics you are so hip!

Mrs. Miller's Magic Trick

I used to tell students to "come up with movement for the poem," which often resulted in a bare minimum effort. Now, I am more specific and say "come up with at least one movement per phrase." By telling them the minimum expectation I usually end up getting a lot, or at least a little, more than the bare minimum!

CoNDuCting WizarDs

Objectives

Students will understand a triple-meter pattern.

Students will be able to show a triple-meter conducting pattern.

Students will identify with music that is used in a cinematic format.

Materials

Recording of "Harry's Wondrous World" by John Williams

Student batons or chopsticks, 1 per student

Spells visuals

Form

Free form

Magic Words

Conductors
Batons

 ## Mrs. Miller's Magic Trick

I am a *huge* Harry Potter fan! (It helps that I live in Orlando and can nerd out at the Harry Potter section of Universal with friends.) For this activity, I borrow a Hogwarts robe and sweater or tie from my even bigger nerd friend, Christina, and go all out with a costume. And instead of using my regular baton (which I do show to the students), I use my Nymphadora Tonks wand that I got at Ollivanders™.

Talk to the students about conductors and the roles they play with orchestras or bands. Perhaps show them a small clip of a vibrant conductor. One of my favorites is Joseph Olefirowicz, the "Dancing Conductor." Sir Simon Rattle is also vibrant on the podium, as is 8-year-old Edward Yudenich. Videos of all three conductors can be found online, though you'll want to review them in advance and select the segment to show, as most are many minutes long.

Connect the movements of these conductors with the movements wizards use to cast spells. You can search online for spell words and create wand moves for each, create your own, or use the provided set of visuals, which includes 12 spell patterns and words is provided for download at www.lorenz.com/resources/magical. They are a mix of lesser-known or foreign-language music vocabulary, composer names, and English-language "thesaurus words" that sound spell like. All provide extension opportunities, and are offered with thanks and credit to my colleagues Sarah Porcenaluk, Aislinn Van Buren, and Christina Torrez.

Pass out the student batons (or chopsticks, rhythm sticks, or whatever you have to use) and have students practice the triple-meter conducting pattern. Observe students to make sure they are executing the gist of the pattern. One of the most common errors is conducting the pattern backwards. As long as students aren't waving their baton frantically, though, I don't nitpick too much.

Choose some of the spells to practice. Students will start at the smiley face and follow the line to the arrow. Have students say the spell name while they do the spell pattern.

Mrs. Miller's Magic Trick

Usually my rule is that we don't talk during the piece, but I do ask students to say the spell names when we are practicing spell movements to get the full effect. Since we are practicing the spell we say it quietly. (We would only yell the spell if we were in battle!) Of course during the triple-meter pattern we say nothing.

Start the music and begin conducting the triple-meter pattern. Once the majority of the students have settled into the pattern, change to a spell. I don't set predetermined points to alternate between the pattern and spells. Rather, I see how well students are performing the pattern and switch when I feel it's appropriate. (I do several dry runs on my own in advance of introducing the lesson to make sure I know the places in the piece where we can switch smoothly.)

This fluidity also allows me to correct any major mistakes students are having. During the conducting portion, I like to go around to students who are not conducting on the steady beat or going completely the wrong way and do some corrections. This always throws off my timing! But because all of the patterns work at any time during the movement and because there really isn't a rigid form to the piece that we have to follow, this is okay. Some classes will perform all of the spells during the song. Others will only get through half of them.

Extension Idea

Divide the class into two groups: conductors and wizards. Conductors are showing off their best triple-meter pattern to the wizards and doing their best conductor impressions. Then the wizards will pick their favorite spells and show them off to the conductors. You can then choose a best wizard and a best conductor from the class!

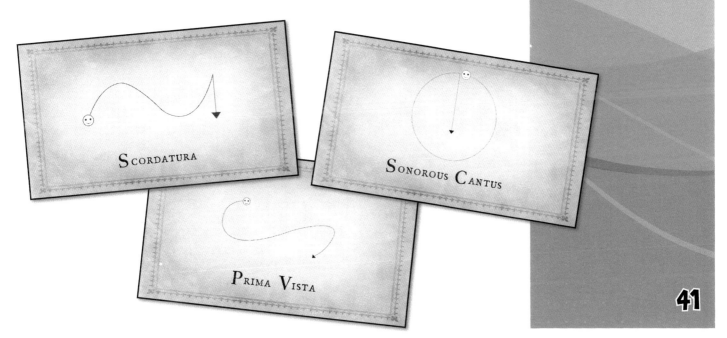

HoeDown Lassos

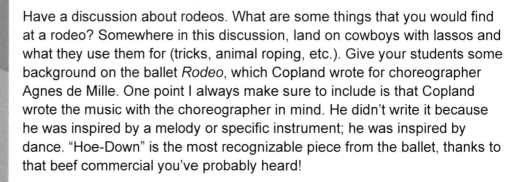

Objectives

Students will be able to identify the form of a piece of music.

Students will listen to ballet music and understand the complementary roles of music and dance in ballet.

Materials

Recording of "Hoe-Down" from *Rodeo* by Aaron Copland

Ribbon streamers

Form map

Form

Introduction–A–B–C–Grand Pause–Interlude–A–Coda

Vocabulary to Use

Form
Melody
Ballet
Choreography

Have a discussion about rodeos. What are some things that you would find at a rodeo? Somewhere in this discussion, land on cowboys with lassos and what they use them for (tricks, animal roping, etc.). Give your students some background on the ballet *Rodeo*, which Copland wrote for choreographer Agnes de Mille. One point I always make sure to include is that Copland wrote the music with the choreographer in mind. He didn't write it because he was inspired by a melody or specific instrument; he was inspired by dance. "Hoe-Down" is the most recognizable piece from the ballet, thanks to that beef commercial you've probably heard!

I set the stage by telling my students that we are cowboys and cowgirls who are going to the hoedown as the entertainment. We will be doing some lasso tricks for the audience!

Mrs. Miller's Magic Trick

I make sure to remind my children that we are cowboys, not Indiana Jones. My children love to whip their ribbon streamers and yes, parts of the movement do ask for the kiddos to "whip up" their streamers. Demonstrate to kiddos that Whip Up is just a quick movement up with their ribbon and *not* one that goes quickly down to create a "whipping" sound. Similarly, when they "throw their lasso" it should be a calculated throw and nothing quick.

There are 13 ribbon moves in the lesson:

Whip Up/Wipers	Move the streamer straight up overhead in one quick motion (beat 1); hold it in the air (beats 2, 3 and 4); then move the streamer on the beat left to right in the air like windshield wipers (beats 5, 6, 7, 8)
Left Circle	Create tight circles on the left side of your body

Right Circle	Create tight circles on the right side of your body
Lasso Circle	Circle the streamer overhead, as if getting ready to lasso something
Throw Lasso	Bring the ribbon streamer quickly to the ground in front of you (beat 1) and hold it there (beats 2, 3 and 4)
Fire/Whip Up	Make small, very fast circles toward the ground (beats 1, 2, 3) then quickly bring the streamer straight up overhead (beat 4)
Big Figure 8	Make an 8-shape in front of the body
Little Figure 8	Make a faster and tighter 8-shape in front of the body
Big Lassos	Giant circles in front of the body
Squiggles	Back and forth in front of the body
Big X	Trace a slow X in front of the body
Flourish Ribbons	Lots of improvisation moves, all in the air
Zorro Move	Make a big "Z" in the air

I benefitted greatly from practicing these first without the kiddos. I also benefitted from some good arm exercises at home and during my planning period to get ready for it. When you're ready, start by practicing these individual movements with your students.

Hoedown Lassos

Introduction – A – B – C – Interlude – A – Coda

Introduction – Practice your lasso moves
A sections – Moves that show your cattle herding skills
B section – Moves that will show how quick you can use your lasso
C section – Moves that will show how fancy you can be with your lasso
Interlude – Improvise lasso moves

This is a long piece with a less-straightforward form and a lot of different melodies. For this activity, I approach the piece in these sections:

Introduction	There's a fairly long introduction (35-40 seconds depending on the recording you use) with one spot to watch out for—about halfway in the orchestra plays the first few notes of the A section before moving into other music. It settles into a quiet "gallop" before A.
A section	First full statement of familiar Hoe-down melody. Listen for the decrescendo to help you transition into the B section.
B section	Quieter section. Melody is played first by the brass then echoed by the woodwinds.
C section	Return to the full orchestra, followed by strings (in a very "hoedown" melody), then some brass and percussion punctuations.
Grand Pause	Approximately two beats
Interlude	Similar material as the introduction but slowing almost to a stop at the end. You will hear the strings come in on a high note to signal that the A section is about to come back.
A section	Starts the same as the opening A section but is shorter.
Coda	The lead-in to the famous "Beef!" tag.

When you're ready to put it together, here are the suggested movements. (If you approach this piece differently, modify the movements to fit that approach.)

Introduction
Improvise lasso tricks!

A section
Whip Up / Wipers (8 counts)
Whip Up / Wipers (8 counts)
Left Circle (8 counts)
Right Circle (8 counts)

Whip Up / Wipers (8 counts)
Whip Up / Wipers (8 counts)
Left Circle (8 counts)
Right Circle (8 counts)

Lasso Circle (4 counts) - You will hear the full orchestra at this point
Throw Lasso (4 counts)
Lasso Circle (4 counts)
Throw Lasso (4 counts)

Whip Up / Wipers (8 counts)
Whip Up / Wipers (8 counts)
Whip Up / Wipers (8 counts)
Continue Wipers until B section begins

B section
Fire / Whip Up (4 counts) - The Whip Up part will match the accented high
    note in the melody.
Fire / Whip Up (4 counts)
Fire / Whip Up (4 counts)

Big Figure 8 (6 counts)
Little Figure 8 (16 counts)

Fire / Whip Up (4 counts)
Fire / Whip Up (4 counts)
Fire / Whip Up (4 counts)
Big Figure 8 (4 counts)

C section
Big Lassos (16 counts)
Squiggles (16 counts)
2 Big X's (8 counts)

Grand Pause
Hand to Ear (so they know it's not over!)

Interlude
Improvise lasso tricks (As tempo slows, the cowboys and cowgirls get tired!)

A section
Whip Up / Wipers (8 counts)
Whip Up / Wipers (8 counts)
Left Circle (8 counts)

Lasso Circle (4 counts) - This is when you hear the full orchestra.
Throw Lasso (4 counts)
Lasso Circle (4 counts)
Throw Lasso (4 counts)

Whip Up / Wipers (8 counts)
Expand Wipers to Flourish Ribbons until Coda begins

Coda
Shout "BEEF!" during final rest
Zorro Move (in time with the last three notes)

Extension Idea
Use this as a performance piece for one of your performance groups. My
kiddos wore cowboy hats and surrounded—with plenty of space—the
audience. It was a huge hit!

Mrs. Miller's Magic Trick

Shouting "BEEF!" is of course optional. However, since I explain to my children that the beef commercials are what make this song so familiar to so many people, I thought it was a good reminder. Plus my kids think it is hilarious!

Kangaroo Expressions

Jumping Kangaroos (A section)

Where's the Joey? (B section)

Percussion Place

Criss Cross Circles

Parachute moves

Mushroom

Washing machine

Little shakes

Digital Files

A complete list of the files available for download at www.lorenz.com/resources/magical follows. You'll also find links to a YouTube playlist of the songs you can use and demo videos of the movements on this webpage. (Note that due to copyright restrictions, the videos show only the movements without audio.)

- **Kangaroo Expressions**
  Form map

- **Lion Long and Short**
  Form map

- **Glow in the Dark Fish**
  Form map

- **Sunshine and Thunder**
  Form map

- **Low and Slow Elephant**
  Form map

- **Mirror Flags**
  Form map

- **Brass Boulevard**
  Form map
  Brass Family visuals

- **Woodwind Way**
  Form map
  Woodwind Family visuals

- **Percussion Place**
  Form map
  Percussion Family visuals
  Cheerleader Dance demo video

- **Strings Street**
  Form map
  String Family visuals

- **Character Collage**
  Form map

- **Sailors' Variations**
  Form map

- **Storm Story**
  Form map

- **Olympic Achievements**
  Form map
  Summer Olympics visuals
  Winter Olympics visuals

- **Conducting Wizards**
  Spells visuals

- **Hoedown Lassos**
  Form map